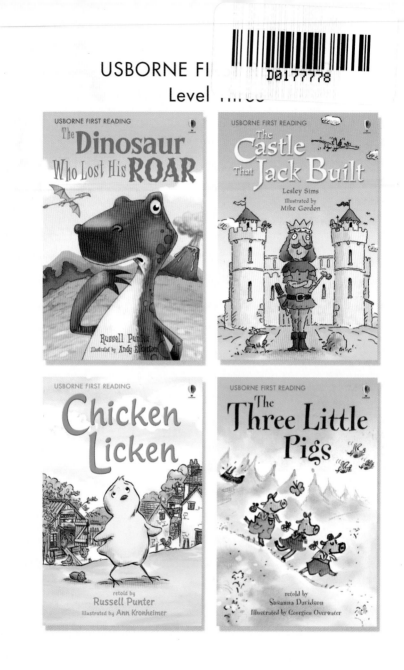

Princess Polly
and the
Pony

Susanna Davidson

Illustrated by Dave Hill

Reading Consultant: Alison Kelly
Roehampton University

Princess Polly
was in trouble.

"You've got **mud** on you!"
cried her father, the King.

"And that's not all," said
her mother, the Queen.

"You've been galloping on
those ponies again!"

"Princesses must not gallop," the King said, crossly. "Ever."

Or canter!

Or trot!

"Being a princess is boring," said Princess Polly.

"I can't do
ANYTHING."

"You could show us your
princess wave," said the Queen.

"Or try on your tiaras?"
said the King.

6

"But no galloping!" they
cried together.

"I know what you can do!"
said the King. "Come to the
Royal Tower."

"I'll show you my crown
collection again."

8

On the way, Princess
Polly spotted a poster.

AMES

g-up Race

y, 9:00am

erry Hill

ges

oyal Wish

"Ooh!" thought Polly. "I wish I could join in."

PONY GAMES

Join in the Dressing-Up Race

Time: Wednesday, 9:00am

Place: Strawberry Hill

For All Ages

First Prize: A Royal Wish

I'd love to be in a race.

The King saw the poster too. "Ah! The race," he said.

"Your mother and I are giving the first prize. Of course, *you* can't enter."

13

"But it's a dressing-up race," thought Princess Polly.

"If I'm in costume, no one will know it's me!"

Princess Polly spent the
next hour looking at her
father's crowns.

The King talked and
talked... and talked.

This crown
belonged to your
Great Aunt Mary...

Polly didn't hear him.
She was thinking about
her costume.

On the day of the race,
Princess Polly jumped out
of bed.

At last!
I can't wait.

She put on her costume...

...and crept outside.

Then she ran all the way to
the royal barn.

Polly climbed onto Pickle,
the smallest pony.

Together they galloped
away to Strawberry Hill.

STRAWBERRY
HILL
THIS WAY
→

Princess Polly got there just
in time. The race was about
to begin.

DRESSING-UP
RACE
STARTS HERE

"One, two, three... GO!"

They were off.

Pickle's hooves pounded
over the ground.

This is fun!

They splashed through
puddles and leaped
over hedges.

"Whoopee!" cried
Princess Polly.

27

The finishing line was getting close. "Slow down, Pickle," said Polly.

"We can't win. My parents
mustn't see me."

But then...

The pony in first place
slipped in some mud...

the pony in second place
couldn't stop in time...

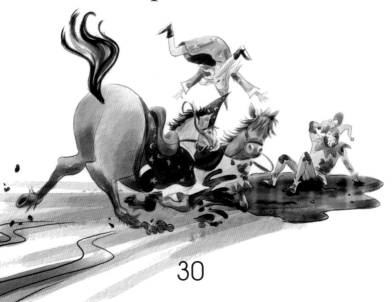

and the pony in third place
crashed into them both.

Princess Polly and Pickle
flew over the finishing line.
They were...

The winners!

"I'll just have to keep my costume on," thought Polly, in a panic.

The Queen had
other ideas.

"Off with your hat and
cloak," she said. "Everyone
wants to see the winner."

"No!" said Princess Polly.
"I want to keep them on."

But the Queen was already
tugging her cloak.

The crowd gasped.
"It's the Princess,"
they cried.

Polly?

"The Princess has won!"
38

"How could you?" said the
Queen. "Look at you!"

"You're *so* muddy. And
your hair is a mess."

39

"You're a disgrace," said the King.

But, as he spoke, the crowd began to cheer.

"Hip hip hooray for
Princess Polly!"

"First prize is a royal wish,"
said a boy. "What are you
going to wish for?"

Princess Polly looked at her parents. "I did win!" she said. "Will you give me a wish?"

"Oh dear!" said the Queen.
"I suppose we must."

What would you like?

A new pink dress?

"For one day each week,
I'd like *not* to be a princess,"
said Polly.

"I want to get muddy and ride ponies and race."

"If you must," said the King, with a sigh.

"But only if you behave like a proper princess for the rest of the time."

"I promise!" said Princess Polly. "But as today is my first non-princess day..."

"I'm going to gallop all the way home!"

Series editor: Lesley Sims

Designed by Louise Flutter

First published in 2007 by Usborne Publishing Ltd., Usborne House,
83-85 Saffron Hill, London EC1N 8RT, England. www.usborne.com
Copyright © 2007 Usborne Publishing Ltd.

All rights reserved. No part of this publication may be reproduced,
stored in a retrieval system or transmitted in any form or by any
means, electronic, mechanical, photocopying, recording or otherwise
without the prior permission of the publisher. The name Usborne
and the devices ♀ ⊕ are Trade Marks of Usborne Publishing Ltd.
Printed in China. UE. First published in America in 2007.

USBORNE FIRST READING
Level Four